For Jinny, for everything—AD
To Remi—MM

Clarion Books
a Houghton Mifflin Company imprint
215 Park Avenue South, New York, NY 10003
Text copyright © 2005 by Alan Durant
Illustrations copyright © 2005 by Mei Matsuoka
First published in Great Britain in 2005 by Andersen Press Ltd.
First American edition, 2006.

The text was set in 19-point BrandoSlab. Text design by David Mackintosh.
The illustrations were executed in colored pencil, acrylics, and cut paper.

Printed in Singapore.

Library of Congress Cataloging-in-Publication Data
Durant, Alan, 1958-
Burger boy / by Alan Durant ; illustrated by Mei Matsuoka.
p. cm.
Summary: Benny hates vegetables and eats nothing but hamburgers, until the day his mother's
prediction proves true and he turns into a walking, talking—and running—burger.
ISBN 0-618-71466-9
[1. Food habits—Fiction. 2. Hamburgers—Fiction. 3. Humorous stories.] I. Matsuoka, Mei, ill. II. Title.
PZ7.D9317Bur 2006
[E]—dc22 2005025363

ISBN-13: 978-0-618-71466-7   ISBN-10: 0-618-71466-9

10 9 8 7 6 5 4 3 2 1

BURGER BOY

by Alan Durant   Illustrated by Mei Matsuoka

Clarion Books

New York

Benny didn't like vegetables.

He didn't like carrots.
He didn't like peas.

He didn't like broccoli or Brussels sprouts,
lettuce, tomato, or cauliflower.

Benny liked burgers. Benny LOVED burgers.
Burgers were the only things Benny would eat.

**"If you don't watch out,
you'll turn into a burger one day,"**

warned his mom.

7

And one day, Benny did.

He and his mother had just finished lunch
at his favorite restaurant, Bigga Burgers,
when a dog ran up and started to sniff him.
"Mmm," said the dog. "Tasty!"
He wagged his tail. He opened his mouth . . .

"Run, Benny, run!" cried Benny's mom.

Benny raced away down the street, with the dog close behind.

"I'm not a burger, I'm a boy!" shouted Benny. "Leave me alone!"

But the dog kept on chasing him,
and soon there were
one, two, three, four, five,
six, seven, eight, nine,
ten dogs,

5

6

4

8

7

10

9

all barking and howling and hounding poor Benny.

11

Benny ran into a field that was full of cows.
"Whew!" he said. "I'll be safe here."

But the cows swished their tails
and crowded around him.

"Don't you know what burgers are made of?" they mooed angrily.

12

"I'm not a burger, I'm a boy!" shouted Benny. "Leave me alone!"

13

Benny took off again,
through the field, across a stream, and down the road,
with the pack of dogs and the herd of cows chasing after him.

Benny saw a group of boys playing ball.
"Help! I'm in trouble. Save me!" he gasped.

The boys stopped playing.
They couldn't believe their eyes.

Their tummies rumbled, and they licked their lips.

"It's burger time!"

they cried.

"I'm not a burger, I'm a boy!" shouted Benny.

"Leave me alone!"

Poor Benny!

Off he ran again, uphill and down, with the pack of dogs,

the herd of cows, and the hungry boys chasing after him.

19

Oh, no!

A busy road blocked Benny's way.

He couldn't go forward.

He couldn't go back.

He was trapped.

Just then, a van screeched to a stop in front of him.
"Need a ride? Quick! Hop in," called the driver.
It was the owner of Bigga Burgers.
"Whew! At last I'm safe," thought Benny
as the van drove away.

But the owner took Benny into Bigga Burgers
and put him on display!

**"Come one, come all.
Only a dollar to see the giant burger!"**
he cried.

"I'm not
a burger,
I'm a boy!"
shouted Benny.
**"Leave me
alone!"**

BIGGA BURGERS

"A talking burger? Even better!"
said the owner.
"I'll charge twice the price."

22

Things were looking bad for Benny.
He was wondering if he'd ever see his home again
when suddenly his mom ran in.

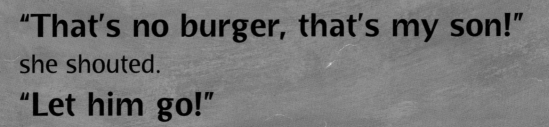

"That's no burger, that's my son!"
she shouted.
"Let him go!"

She took Benny home

and fed him fruits
and vegetables.

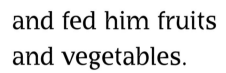

Slowly, his burger body
turned boyish at the edges,
and finally he was back
to his old shape again.

"**Hooray! I'm cured!**"
cried Benny.

"**I'll never eat
another burger.**"

And he didn't.

He ate carrots and peas, broccoli and Brussels sprouts, lettuce, tomato, and cauliflower.

Now Benny liked vegetables. He LOVED vegetables. Vegetables were the only things he'd eat.

His mother was worried.

"Benny," she said, "you'd better watch out.
If all you eat is vegetables, one day . . .

. . . you'll turn into one!"